HOW MANY MILES TO
BETHLEHEM?

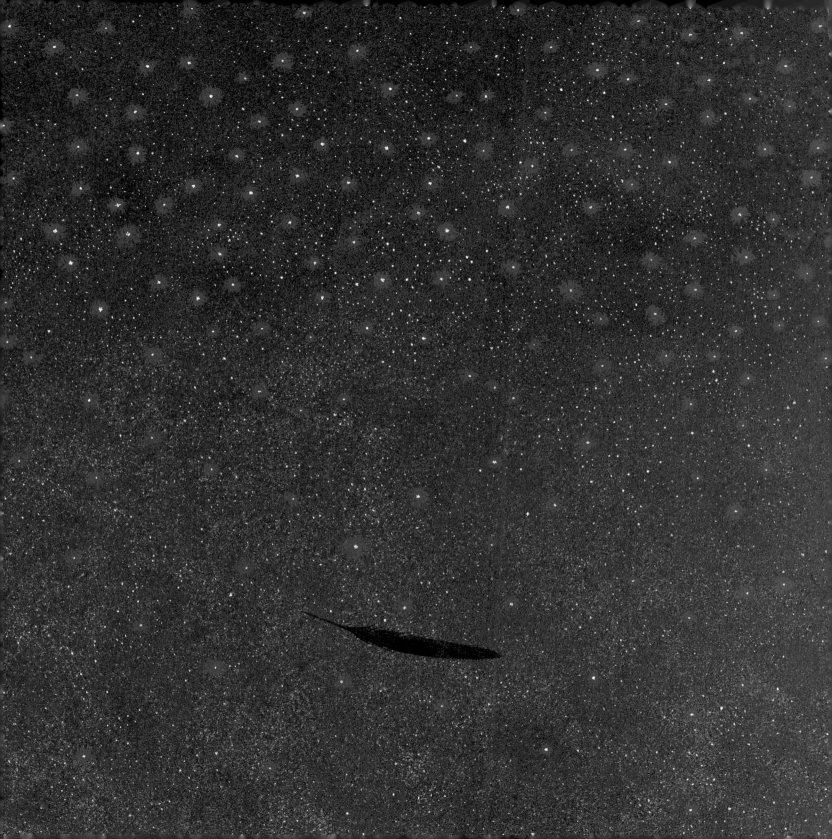

TO PHOEBE, IMOGEN, AND THEIR RABBIT, FLOPSY

——P. M.

ISBN 0-439-72063-X

Text copyright © 2004 by Kevin Crossley-Holland. Illustrations copyright © 2004 by Peter Malone. All rights reserved. Published by Scholastic Inc., by arrangement with Orion Children's Books. SCHOLASTIC and the LANTERN LOGO are trademarks and/or registered trademarks of Scholastic Inc.

Arthur A. Levine Books hardcover edition published by Arthur A. Levine Books, an imprint of Scholastic Inc., October 2004.

12 11 10 9 8 7 6 5 4 3 2 1   4 5 6 7 8 9/0

Printed in the U.S.A.   40

First Scholastic paperback printing, November 2004

HOW MANY MILES TO
BETHLEHEM?

KEVIN CROSSLEY-HOLLAND ✸ *Illustrated by* PETER MALONE

SCHOLASTIC INC.
New York Toronto London Auckland Sydney
Mexico City New Delhi Hong Kong Buenos Aires

I AM MARY. Tight as a drum. Round as the lady moon calling out to me. We're so far from home, and my baby will be born tonight.

Where can I lie down?
Joseph has gone up to ask the innkeeper.

I'M THE INNKEEPER.

Sorry, Joseph! Every space is taken, and there's nothing left to eat — I'm even out of figs and grapes.

We'll all be hungry tonight. My guests. My cats. Everyone except the stone-hearted Emperor.

I tell you what. Here's a light! Your Mary can share a stall with my old ox.

I'M THE OX, and I keep yawning. My master works me so hard. There's not much hay in here, Mary. You'll be better off with the silly donkey.

I'M THE DONKEY. I'm not silly!

You can stay here, Mary. Hey! Do you want a mouthful of my straw and barley?

At least you'll be warm in my stall. Better than in the dark and the damp with the wandering shepherds.

W E'RE THE SHEPHERDS. There was this light in the night-sky and the old moon herself went white. And there was a sky-voice saying, "Jesus, the lamb of God, will be born tonight. You'll find him in Bethlehem, lying in a manger."

Then this whole flock of lights skips around us. "Peace on earth," they sing. "Follow the brightest star."

I AM THE BRIGHTEST STAR. Night-sky's many-colored flower, opening over Bethlehem.

Follow me.

I bring hope in the darkness. Hope to the wandering shepherds. Hope to wise men.

WE ARE THREE WISE MEN, Caspar and Melchior and Balthasar. We're riding from Arabia.

We saw the star in the east, scarlet as a sky-anemone, golden as a mustard-flower. We understood.

W hen we reach Jerusalem, we'll tell King Herod we wish to kneel to Jesus, child and king.

N<small>O!</small> I <small>AM THE KING.</small> Herod the king. I've told those three travellers from Arabia I too will kneel to Jesus; but as soon as they tell me where to find him, I'll rip him away from his mother.

I AM THE MOTHER, MARY.
My little lamb! My perfect stranger!
   I'll wrap you with these swaddling bands.
I'll lay you in this manger.
   This is my child.

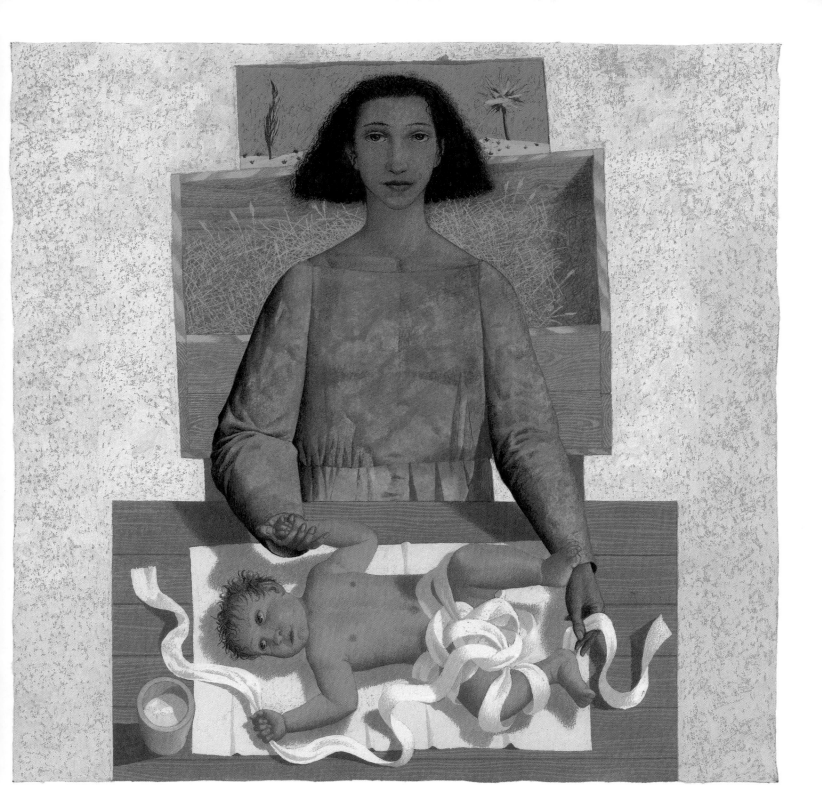

I AM THE CHILD AND KING. Lord of locusts and wild honey, and the lemon groves. I am the Shepherd and the Lamb.

I'M A LAMB TOO, and I've trotted all the way here with my brothers and sisters. The dancing star guided us. Look! We've brought along our shepherds.

W E'RE THE SHEPHERDS. What a journey! The tent of the sky swaying, the earth's bones shaking. Shining pebbles hopping and clapping around our feet.

Little Jesus, here's a fleece. A round of ewe's cheese. And a palm fan. That's all we have. We're only poor shepherds. We're not rich or wise.

WE ARE THE WISE MEN. Imagine! The son of God born in a stable. Royal gold and priestly frankincense, and bitter myrrh. These are our gifts to you.

Herod the king is jealous and afraid. You are in great danger. We must all escape.

Little Jesus, may your angels lead us.

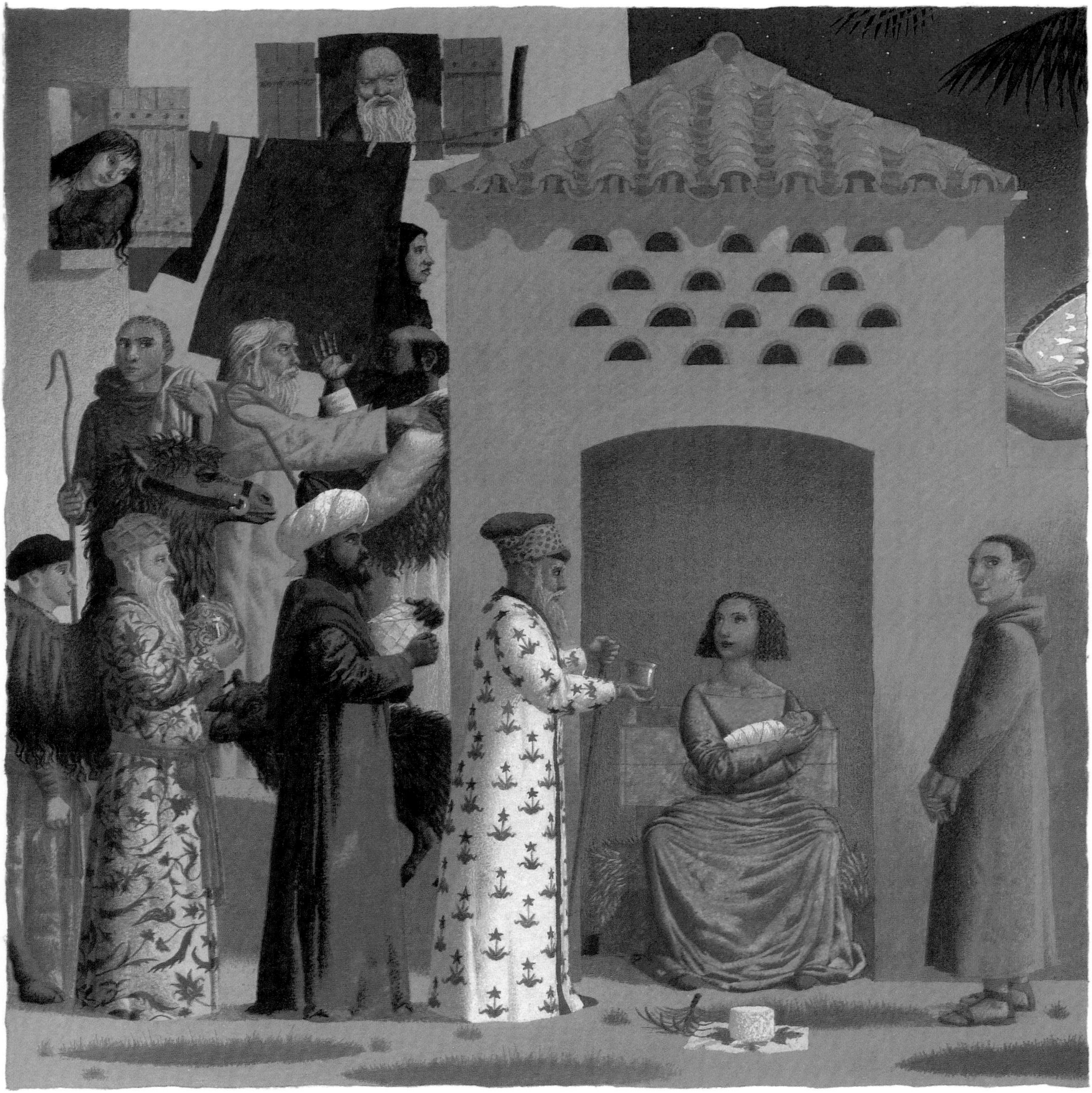

W E ARE ANGELS. We are your secret voices. Listen!

"This baby!"

"Rejoice!"

"This hope!"

"This peace!"

Wandering shepherds, wise men, we will enfold you.

We will lead Mary and Joseph with our light.

I AM THE LIGHT OF LIGHT. The baby who will cradle the world. In your heart, hold me. I will never leave you.

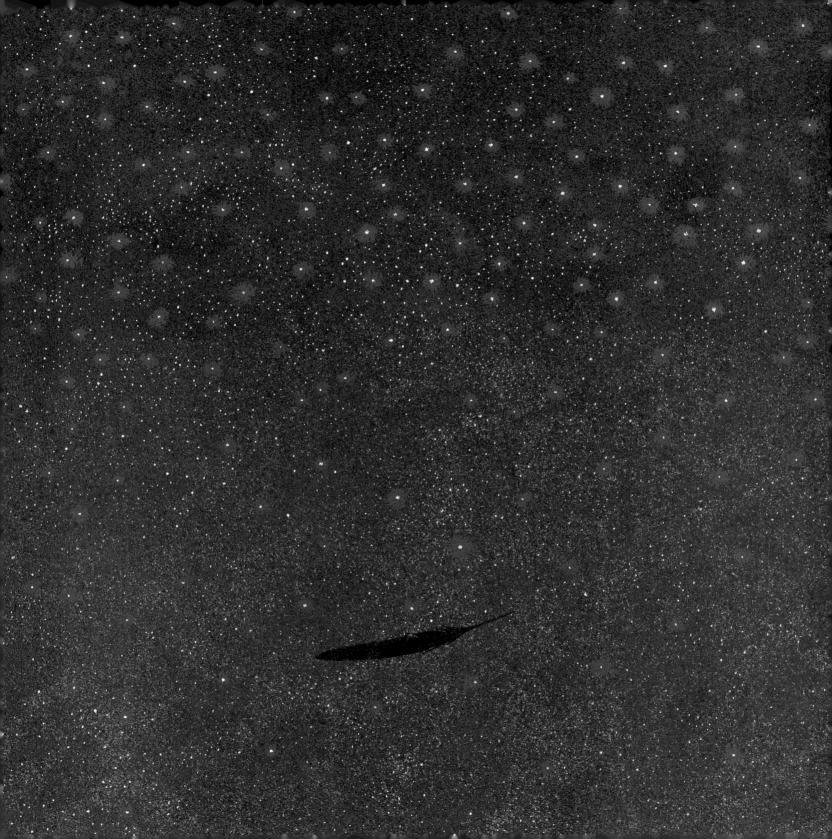